BASEBALL FEVER

OTHER YEARLING BOOKS YOU WILL ENJOY:

UPCHUCK SUMMER, *Joel L. Schwartz*
HENRY AND THE PAPER ROUTE, *Beverly Cleary*
HENRY AND THE CLUBHOUSE, *Beverly Cleary*
HENRY AND RIBSY, *Beverly Cleary*
HENRY HUGGINS, *Beverly Cleary*
JELLY BELLY, *Robert Kimmel Smith*
SOUP, *Robert Newton Peck*
SOUP AND ME, *Robert Newton Peck*
SOUP FOR PRESIDENT, *Robert Newton Peck*

YEARLING BOOKS/YOUNG YEARLINGS/YEARLING CLASSICS are designed especially to entertain and enlighten young people. Patricia Reilly Giff, consultant to this series, received the bachelor's degree from Marymount College. She holds the master's degree in history from St. John's University, and a Professional Diploma in Reading from Hofstra University. She was a teacher and reading consultant for many years, and is the author of numerous books for young readers.

For a complete listing of all Yearling titles, write to
Dell Readers Service, P.O. Box 1045,
South Holland, IL 60473.

JOHANNA HURWITZ

Baseball Fever

ILLUSTRATED BY RAY CRUZ

A YEARLING BOOK

Published by
Dell Publishing
a division of
The Bantam Doubleday Dell Publishing Group, Inc.
666 Fifth Avenue
New York, New York 10103

ISBN: 0-440-40311-1

Reprinted by arrangement with William Morrow and Company, Inc.
Printed in the United States of America

March 1983

20 19 18 17 16 15 14 13 12

CW

For Isadora, Steve, Lisa, and Daniel Kunitz,
because they like baseball
and because I like them.

The author wishes to thank two ardent and knowledgeable baseball enthusiasts without whom this book could never have been written:

Ben Hurwitz (Yankee fan)
Nomi Hurwitz (Mets fan)

CONTENTS

BASEBALL FEVER

1

INTRODUCING EZRA

Ezra Feldman's father knew six different languages. He had a doctorate in history, and he could do hard arithmetic problems in his head. His hobbies were reading history and sociology books. He had a photographic memory and could play a whole chess game without using a board. He just moved the pieces around inside his head. In short, he understood all sorts of long and complicated things. But there were two things he didn't understand at all. He didn't understand Ezra, and he didn't understand baseball.

Ezra was almost ten years old, and he liked baseball more than anything else in the world. He listened to baseball games on the radio, and he watched baseball games on television. When he read books, they were books about baseball. When he talked, he talked a lot about baseball. At night when he slept, he often dreamed about baseball.

"Ezra would eat and drink baseball if he could," his mother said laughingly.

"Why do you want to look at that?" Mr. Feldman would ask, whenever he saw his son entranced before a baseball game on TV. "That's nothing but a lot of grown men taking turns hitting a ball with a stick. What a waste of time!" he complained. He had no patience for any sports.

Ezra had an older brother named Harris. He was nineteen years old and away at college. When Harris was nine, going on ten, he hadn't been interested in baseball. He had spent his time doing experiments with his chemistry set, and by the time Harris was ten he had memorized the entire periodic table. Mr. Feldman couldn't understand how two boys with the same parents could be so different.

"Don't forget, we didn't live in Flushing when Harris was young," Mrs. Feldman reminded her husband. Flushing was where Ezra lived, and it was also the home of Ezra's favorite team, the New York Mets. Shea Stadium, where they played, was within walking distance from the house Ezra's parents had bought four years before. Harris had spent his formative years in Mahwah, New Jersey, where there was no baseball team.

A typical conversation between Ezra and his father went this way:

"Dad, watch out! You're blocking the TV screen. The bases are loaded, and there are two men out. The man at the plate has three balls and two strikes. This is the payoff pitch coming up."

"I can't understand a word you're saying," Mr. Feldman would grumble. "Why should a boy your age sit around watching grown men acting like fools? It's ridiculous!"

Ezra groaned, partly because his father continued to block the television screen and partly because the man at bat had struck out.

Even though he had explained them to him a hundred times, his father kept forgetting the rules of baseball. He still insisted that RBI meant "rubbish brought inside." He couldn't remember "runs batted in." And if Ezra told him that somebody hit a double, Mr. Feldman always asked, "Does that mean they got two points?" Ezra didn't know how a person who could read ancient Greek could be that dumb.

Mrs. Feldman said it was because Ezra's father had grown up in Europe, where baseball is not a popular sport. Mr. Feldman had been born in Germany and had been sent to England before the Second World War. After the war he came to the United States, but it was too late. "I think you have to be born in America to appreciate baseball," Mrs. Feldman explained to her son. "It's the same with pumpkin pie." Indeed, Mr. Feldman didn't like pumpkin pie either, and both Ezra and his mother loved it. Even Harris, born in Chicago and raised in New Jersey, liked pumpkin pie despite his indifference to baseball.

Pumpkin pies came in the fall, just when the baseball season was ending. They were a small compensation. But Ezra kept watching the calendar and counting the days until February. In February, spring training began, and the newspapers would be filled with more baseball information.

Ezra's favorite month of the year was April when the baseball season opened and his birthday occurred. His birthday was April first, and the baseball season usually opened a few days later.

"April is when the income tax is due," Mr. Feldman would remember. He forgot the new baseball season, but at least he remembered the taxes and his son's birthday. Two and a half weeks before Ezra's tenth birthday, his father came home with an early gift, an electronic chess game for them to share. But sharing a chess game wasn't like sharing a pumpkin pie with his mother. For one thing, Mr. Feldman played with the chess game much more than his son did. Ezra understood the basic rules of chess, but the game wasn't exciting like baseball. Besides, when he played chess with his father, he always knew the outcome of the game in advance. Mr. Feldman won every time.

"You have to lose a lot of games and understand the reasons why you lost before you can win," his father explained. Unfortunately, instead of being encouraged, Ezra found this information more discouraging than ever.

"What's the matter with you?" complained Mr. Feldman. "Harris was beating me when he was your age."

"Ezra is just as smart as Harris, in his own way," Mrs. Feldman said, defending their son. "Someday he'll surprise us. Just be patient."

Mrs. Feldman was a radiologist, and at work she was called Dr. Feldman. She worked much longer hours at North Shore Hospital than Mr. Feldman (who was also called Dr. Feldman) worked at Queens College, where he taught. When she came home, she relaxed by listening to classical music on the stereo. She also liked to do crossword puzzles. She was quite good at them, but she could never have finished a puzzle without the assistance of her husband and son. If she needed to know the name of an ancient king or some obscure character in mythology, Mr. Feldman always knew the answer. And whenever there was a clue relating to baseball, she could rely on Ezra to know the answer.

"I need a four-letter name of a baseball player. The third letter is Y," Mrs. Feldman might shout. That was so easy that Ezra didn't even have to take time out to think.

"Willie Mays," he'd call back. "He played on the Giants, and he hit 660 home runs in his career. He also played on the Mets and. . . ."

"Stop," Mrs. Feldman would shout back. "All I need is M-a-y-s."

Obviously, Mrs. Feldman wasn't a baseball fan, or she would have been able to answer a question as simple as that one. But though she didn't follow the sport, she did have some understanding of Ezra's obsession with it. Her brother, Ezra's Uncle Edward in Chicago, had always loved football. She remembered how he had watched games on television, even refusing to come for meals, when he was young. Uncle Edward was now a successful surgeon. Football had not impaired his brains or his life, and she knew that Ezra would survive baseball. Mrs. Feldman was also tolerant of such related passions as collecting baseball cards.

"What are those?" Mr. Feldman had asked, when he first noticed his son sorting a shoe box filled with cards. Mr. Feldman was disgusted when he heard the answer. "Why can't you collect something worthwhile, like stamps or coins?" he asked. "You can learn a lot from them, and someday they will be worth a great deal of money."

"I learn a lot from baseball cards, and besides a hard-to-get baseball card can sell for a couple of hundred dollars," Ezra protested.

"What kind of values does your country

have?" Mr. Feldman asked, turning to his wife.

"It's your country now too, dear," Mrs. Feldman reminded him.

"Don't worry about it, Dad," said Ezra. "I never chew the gum that comes with the cards. I throw it out."

"You mean to say that you get chewing gum with these cards, and you don't use it? What kind of waste goes on here?"

"These are my cavity-prone years," Ezra reminded his father. "You wouldn't want me to chew one hundred packages of gum, would you?"

"One hundred packages!"

"Well, actually, by the end of the baseball season it will be a lot more."

"Baseball." Mr. Feldman shuddered. "It's like a disease with you. I just can't understand it."

"I guess I've got baseball fever, just the way they say on the TV commercials," said Ezra.

"I hope you recover one of these days," said Mr. Feldman.

"I'll never recover," said Ezra with certainty. "I like it too much."

He could not possibly make his father understand.

2

A LITTLE COACHING FROM HARRIS

Two weeks before his tenth birthday and three weeks before the start of the baseball season, Ezra went to spend the weekend in Princeton. Harris had been promising to invite him, and now that he shared an apartment with a couple of other fellows instead of living in the dormitory, he could more easily arrange to have a visitor. Mr. Feldman drove Ezra to the bus terminal.

"Before you know it, you'll be going off to college yourself," Mr. Feldman said.

"I'm only in fourth grade," Ezra protested.

"Well, it goes awfully fast. It seems like yesterday that Harris was in fourth grade too."

Ezra laughed. He had been born when Harris was in fourth grade. To Ezra, it seemed like ages ago, not yesterday.

"Have a good time," Mr. Feldman told his son. "Tell Harris about the chess computer I bought for us. He'll enjoy playing with it when he comes home again."

Harris met Ezra at the bus station in Princeton and took him to the apartment, which was actually a basement in a private house. He showed Ezra where he would sleep, on a lumpy sofa that had been inherited from the previous occupants of the apartment. "It isn't as luxurious as home," Harris apologized, "but it's nicer than living in the dorm."

"Do you cook your own food?" Ezra wanted to know.

"Some," said Harris. "Mostly we just open cans or eat hamburgers. I was discussing with Bob and Roger where you and I should have supper." Bob and Roger were his roommates. "Bob says that Gino's pizza is the best. Roger said that we should go to Elio's. So guess what I decided?"

"That we'll have hamburgers at McDonald's?" Ezra offered.

"No." Harris grinned. "We'll order a small pie at Gino's, and then we'll order a small pie at Elio's. Then *you* can judge which is the best."

"Sure," said Ezra.

"There's a good movie playing in town tonight," Harris went on. "I thought we'd go."

"Sure," said Ezra. He didn't care what they did. Just being with Harris made him feel good. He admired his older brother more than he admired anyone else he knew, outside the field of baseball. Even though Harris didn't care for baseball, however, he seemed to understand Ezra's interest in it in a way their father couldn't.

They drove to the pizza parlor in Harris's old car. It was a '66 Dodge, and he had bought it the previous June from a graduating senior.

The odometer had already clocked 142,000 miles, and Harris explained that his goal was to reach 200,000 before he graduated.

"Sure," said Ezra, "if it doesn't break down. But when will you have time to study?"

"Junior year isn't so hard," Harris explained. "The tough time is when you're a freshman. Then it gets easier."

Ezra wondered if what he said was really true. Harris was very smart. Easy for him might be tough for someone else.

"So, how is life treating you?" Harris asked, as they bit into their first slices of Gino's pizza.

"OK," said Ezra, shrugging his shoulders. "But I'm getting ready for rough times ahead."

"What's the problem?" asked Harris.

"*I* don't have a problem," said Ezra, "but Dad does." He swallowed the pizza and felt the burned roof of his mouth with his tongue. Too bad it was impossible to eat pizza without burning one's mouth on the first bite every time.

"The baseball season is about to begin, and you know how mad Dad gets when I watch the games. He says it's just a waste of time," Ezra explained.

"I guess I was lucky not to be a baseball freak like you," said Harris. "I never had that problem."

"You weren't lucky," said Ezra. "Baseball is one of the best things in the world. I like it more than anything. I just wish it didn't make Dad angry when I watch the games."

"It's because he cares for you so much," Harris said. "He knows you have a first-class mind, and he worries that you're not realizing your potential. All fathers are like that. They want their children to get the Nobel Prize before they're fifteen. But so far, no fifteen-year-old has succeeded."

"What's the Nobel Prize?" asked Ezra.

"It's a lot of money and a lot of honor," explained Harris. "Sort of like winning a super World Series," he said.

"How come Mom doesn't make a fuss?" asked Ezra. "Doesn't she want me to win the Nobel Prize too?"

"Mom has a different temperament. She *knows* you'll win the Nobel Prize—after me, of course. You'll have to wait about ten years so people don't say there was nepotism involved. Anyhow, she knows that you'll do OK, so she leaves you alone. She left me alone when Dad was on my back too."

"When was Dad ever on your back?" asked Ezra. He had only heard his father praise his oldest son. He couldn't imagine him scolding Harris about anything.

"You were too little to notice, probably three or four years old. I built a laboratory in my bedroom. We didn't live in the big house in Flushing then. I had a tiny room by the kitchen, and it always smelled of chemicals. Dad said it stank. He thought I would inhale poison gas and kill myself. He was always trying to get me to go outdoors and breathe fresh air."

YORK
APARTMTS
WANTED
HALL

Ezra laughed. "He's always after me to stay inside and read a book by Alexander Dumas or someone."

"You ought to try. *The Count of Monte Cristo* is a good one," Harris said. "But anyhow, I remember that in those days Dad and I were always arguing."

"When did you stop?" asked Ezra.

"Gradually we both learned to compromise. I made a bargain with him. If he let me work with my chemicals for a couple of hours every day, then I would spend some time outside. That's when I started running. I began jogging before they were selling jogging suits and it was the in thing to do. Imagine, I used to run three or four miles every day in jeans and tennis sneakers. Nowadays they would probably arrest a person who did that." Harris grinned. He was on the cross-country team, and even though he planned to drive 58,000 miles in the next year or so, he also planned to run in the New York Marathon.

"The problem is that Dad is home too

much," said Ezra. "Unless he has a department meeting or a conference with a student, he gets home from work even before I'm home from school. He's home all summer, and vacation starts for him in May and doesn't end till the middle of September. That's practically the whole baseball season. If he worked like the fathers of the others kids I know, he wouldn't be around when I was watching or listening to a lot of the games. He has that big room as a study, but instead of staying inside he's always walking around the house."

"Just because he doesn't have a nine-to-five job, you talk as if Dad sat home all day and did nothing but watch you. He does teach three college courses a semester, and he is in the middle of writing his third book," Harris reminded Ezra.

"I know." Ezra sighed. "But somehow every time I turn on the television set, there Dad is, looking at me."

Harris nodded sympathetically.

"What do you think I should do?" Ezra

asked, as they got into the car and drove to Elio's for the completion of their meal. Harris gave the matter some thought. Not until he was on his second slice of their second pizza did he come up with a suggestion. "You could make a bargain with Dad. You were telling me about the chess computer before. Well, if you could beat Dad in a couple of games, it would prove to him that your brains haven't atrophied from all that baseball. And if you beat him at chess, you would be in a much stronger position to get him to let you watch the games. Why don't you make a deal with him to let you watch all the games you want, if you can beat him at chess?"

"If I could get him to take me to a live game, it would be even better," said Ezra. "Maybe then he'd feel the excitement of baseball and understand it more. And besides, I'll miss too much of the season if I can't watch games until I beat him."

"OK. Do it that way. I bet it will work. Anyway, it would really please Dad if you offered to play him from time to time," Harris said.

Ezra finished his share of the pizza slices. He was too full to appreciate the difference between the two stores. Luckily, Harris didn't ask him to evaluate them. He thought about what his brother had said. He wondered if it would really work. He'd have to think about it some more, he decided. The deal wouldn't be worth it if he had to play a hundred games of chess with his father and never won a single one.

Harris took Ezra to a Woody Allen movie. Ezra had seen it once already, but it was still funny. Actually, it was even funnier this time, because there were a lot of jokes that Ezra had missed the first time around. I guess I'm getting older, Ezra thought proudly. But it wasn't his understanding of the sophisticated jokes or his approaching birthday that made him feel so grown up. It was the man-to-man talk with Harris. Too bad Harris wasn't his father, he thought.

8

EZRA'S BIRTHDAY

To celebrate Ezra's tenth birthday, his parents invited his friends Bruce and Louis, who were twins, out to dinner with them on April first. They were going to eat at Chopmeat Charlie's. Ezra's parents liked Chopmeat Charlie's because it sold good-quality steaks and chops and because it had a "kiddy special" for children under twelve. For a flat rate of three dollars each, the boys could have all the salad they could eat, a quarter-pound hamburger with French fries, all the soda they could drink, and a scoop of ice cream for dessert. It was a bargain.

"I wish I could pass for under twelve," Mr. Feldman said every single time they ate there. Ezra didn't feel that way. Even though his parents could afford it, he wouldn't be permitted to order a steak until he had outgrown the "kiddy special," which meant two more years of hamburgers. A bargain was too important to be turned down. Nevertheless, both Bruce and Louis were very impressed with the restaurant.

Ezra realized that he ate out in restaurants more often than his friends. Since Mrs. Feldman worked long hours, she frequently didn't have time to cook dinner. Ezra was proud of his mother and her important job at the hospital, so he didn't mind that he wasn't having a more traditional party at home. But he hoped that his father wouldn't say anything foolish during the evening. Mr. Feldman didn't really know how to make conversation with fourth-grade boys any more than he had known how to make conversation with third-grade boys the year before.

Almost immediately the evening started off wrong. "Did you hear about Lee Mazzilli?" asked Louis. "He broke his finger."

"Oh, no!" said Ezra. "That's awful!"

"Is that one of your classmates?" asked Mr. Feldman. "Don't worry. He won't have to miss any school. They'll just put a splint on his finger, and he'll be back tomorrow."

"Oh, Dad," said Ezra. "He's not at school. He's a player for the Mets, and if he broke his finger he won't be able to play."

"April Fool!" shouted Louis. "Lee Mazzilli didn't break anything."

Everyone laughed. But Ezra was embarrassed. Everyone else's father knew who Lee Mazzilli was.

"I think they've traded for a new southpaw," said Bruce. "But I forgot his name. They sure can use one."

"A southpaw?" asked Mr. Feldman. "How about a westpaw?"

"A southpaw is a left-handed pitcher," Ezra explained. He had given his father information of this sort a dozen times over the last couple of years. "There's no such thing as a westpaw."

"Let's go help ourselves to salad," said Ezra. The sooner they were eating, the better. Bruce and Louis heaped their plates with everything. Since Ezra had eaten here before, he knew just how much his stomach could hold. But Bruce and Louis were new to the opportunities of the unlimited salad bar, and they took mounds of everything.

Mr. Feldman cut slices of French bread and pumpernickel and brought them to their table. The boys started eating. If everyone's mouth was filled with food, there wouldn't be so much talking, Ezra reasoned. But Mr. Feldman seemed to want to keep the conversation going.

"Read any good books lately?" he asked his son's friends.

"Nope," said Bruce between mouthfuls of salad. "I read one for a book report, but it was awful. Now I don't have to read anything till the next report next month."

"You should try *The Three Musketeers* and *The Hunchback of Notre Dame,*" said Ezra's father. He was always recommending those books to his son too. "And you ought to look into Jules Verne. I loved his books when I was your age."

"He wrote *Journey to the Center of the Earth,* didn't he?" asked Louis, stuffing a cherry tomato into his mouth.

Mr. Feldman brightened. "Ah, so you are a reader!" he said, smiling.

"Oh, no. I saw it on TV."

"Doesn't seeing it make you want to read the book?" asked Mr. Feldman.

"No. I only watched it because a ball game was rained out and they showed that instead.

I'd rather watch a game any day," said Louis.

That ended conversation for a little while. Bruce and Louis finished every bit of the salad they had taken. Louis even went back for more.

"I had eighteen olives," said Bruce, counting the pits. "That's a record for me. My mother never lets me have so many."

"I don't like olives," said Louis. "But I bet I ate over a hundred chick-peas. I should have counted."

"Well, don't overdo a good thing, fellows," said Mrs. Feldman. "I don't want you boys to get sick."

"That's OK, Mrs. Feldman," said Louis. "You're a doctor. You can cure us." He ate a third slice of French bread.

The waitress took the empty salad plates and brought the three hamburgers and French fries. Ezra's parents had both ordered steak.

While he waited for his turn at the ketchup, Ezra thought about his birthday gifts. Harris had given him a copy of *The Baseball Encyclopedia* when he had visited him at Princeton. That was something he had wanted for a long time. The twins had given him an envelope. Inside was a box-seat ticket to a Mets doubleheader in May. Bruce and Louis and their father would be going too, even though the twins' birthday wasn't until next September.

"This root beer is great," said Bruce, draining his second glass. "I've never had enough root beer in my life." He poured himself another glass from the pitcher on the table.

"Either of you fellows play chess?" asked Mr. Feldman. "You could play a game on the electronic chess game that Ezra got for his birthday."

Ezra made a face. Everyone made out very well on *his* birthday, he thought. Bruce and Louis and their father were going to a baseball game, his parents were eating steak, his friends were making pigs of themselves, and his father had bought him an electronic chess set that he wanted and Ezra didn't. Now he could be beaten by a machine as well as by his father.

"These French fries are great," said Louis. "Do you think they will give us some more?"

"When was the last time you fellows ate?" asked Mrs. Feldman.

"Not since our after-school snack," answered Bruce, taking another bite out of his hamburger.

Mr. Feldman returned to his subject. "Well, wait till you see the electronic chess set," he said. "It's amazing what science can do. You push a switch, and that little box can make some brilliant moves. I played three games this afternoon."

"Excuse me," said Bruce, jumping up from the table.

"Is everything all right?" asked Mrs. Feldman. She didn't need her medical eye to see that something was wrong.

"Which way is the bathroom?" asked Bruce.

He was looking slightly green. Ezra won-

dered if the color was from the greenness of the olives or the two pickles that Bruce had eaten with his hamburger.

"Come," said Mr. Feldman. He leaped up and took Bruce by the arm. They were gone for several minutes.

"My father said that you shouldn't worry about our game being rained out," said Louis, eating French fries from his brother's plate. "If it rains that day, he said he'll take us to a different game with the same box seats!"

"Good," said Ezra. He thought Louis was beginning to look a little green now too.

Bruce returned to the table. His color was much better. He looked at the remaining piece of hamburger on his plate.

"Are you sure you should continue eating?" asked Mrs. Feldman.

"Why not?" asked Mr. Feldman sarcastically. "He has plenty of room *now*."

Then Louis jumped up. His eyes seemed to be bulging from their sockets. "Which way is the bathroom?" he gasped.

"Oh, no!" cried Mr. Feldman with a groan. "Not another one! They won't let us return here again."

He rushed off in the direction of the men's room, pulling Louis with him.

Ezra looked down at his plate. Thank goodness he wouldn't have another birthday for a long time. One a year was plenty. Now all he wanted was to go home and continue studying his baseball encyclopedia. There were a lot of things he wanted to learn.

4

THE NEW SEASON

Mrs. Feldman usually left for work in the morning before her husband and son. So the two of them sat at the breakfast table together with the newspaper between them. While Mr. Feldman read about the troubles in the world on the front pages, Ezra read the section with the sports news. The arrangement was a good one, and at such times Ezra thought perhaps it was for the best that he and his father each had their separate interests on separate pages.

Once Ezra's birthday was over, there were

not many days to wait until the baseball season began. The contracts were signed, trades had been made from one team to another, spring training was concluded, and the new season was ready to begin.

As a team, the New York Mets had suffered a lot of bad luck the year before. There had been many injuries to good players and a couple of poor trades. They hadn't played well, but even though they lost more games than they won, Ezra remained loyal to them. A new season meant a new start. Ezra was convinced that they would do much better this year.

Ezra came home from school on Friday, April eighth, and dropped his books on the living-room floor. He had just survived the longest afternoon of his life, waiting for school to be dismissed. This was the day of the first Met game of the season, and even though the Mets were playing right here in Flushing, his teacher had not been at all interested. Louis turned on his little transistor radio softly at two o'clock when the game began without attracting her attention. The class was having a silent reading period and so all was quiet. Unexpectedly the volume on the radio went up, and the strains of "The Star Spangled Banner" could be heard in the classroom. Half the class jumped to attention and began to sing as they had been taught. Instead of being proud of her class's patriotism, Ezra's teacher confiscated the radio and gave them all a written assignment.

But at last he was free to turn on the television and watch the game. How lucky he was that for once his father wasn't home to complain about it. The picture took a few seconds to come into focus, but the sound began instantly. A happy feeling came over Ezra as he listened to the noise of the crowd. He imagined himself sitting in the stadium too. He wished he could someday make his father understand the wonderful feeling of excitement he felt whenever a new game began. He never knew what would happen, and it was

like his birthday or Christmas each time: maybe good surprises, maybe disappointments, but always something to keep him guessing.

Ezra loved the ease with which the players moved. His mother had once taken him to see the ballet, and he thought the dancers leaped into the air just like baseball players jumping for high fly balls. One of the reasons he didn't like the Little League teams was that no one could play with the smoothness and authority of the professional players. If someone hit the ball well, someone else would drop it. If someone made a good catch, someone else would throw the ball poorly. The professional baseball players rarely made such foolish moves. Ezra knew that many people thought the Mets were a bad team. But he was proud of them. After all, the game that he was watching was less than a mile away. They were his neighbors, and he felt a responsibility to watch and to cheer for them.

The announcer's voice said that this was the

bottom of the fourth inning and the game was tied two-two. It was going to be close, and Ezra was sure his team would win. It would be a great way to start off the new season.

The fourth inning ended and the fifth too, and the score remained the same. In the sixth inning, the Chicago Cubs got two hits and there were no men out. Ezra sat on the edge of the sofa and held his breath. Suddenly the phone rang. He jumped.

"Hello," he said, trying to listen to the sportscaster with one ear and the voice on the phone with the other. As a result, he understood neither.

"Ezra," said his father's voice. "I'm at work and I need a forty-cent airmail stamp. It's very important. Walk over to the post office and pick one up for me right away. No, wait. Better get two. This letter may be thick."

"OK," said Ezra. "Two stamps." He tried to hear the sportscaster for a moment. He heard some cheers, but he didn't know if they meant someone had scored a run or if the Cubs were retired.

"Not just any stamps," said Mr. Feldman. "Airmail. Do you understand? Do you have money?"

"Yes. Yes," said Ezra. He was in a hurry to hang up the phone and find out what had happened at the game.

"Two airmail stamps. Don't forget!" said Mr. Feldman, as he hung up.

Ezra went back to look at the television. While he had been discussing postage stamps the Chicago Cubs had scored a run. Now they were ahead three to two. Ezra couldn't leave at this point. He glanced at his wristwatch. It was 3:55. He still had plenty of time to get the stamps. Unlike a chess game where one wrong move could be decisive, a baseball game wasn't over until the last pitch.

He sat down again and watched. "Come on," he encouraged each Met, as he came to bat. "You can do it."

But though there were some long line

drives, they all seemed to be going foul. It must be the way the wind is blowing today, thought Ezra.

Finally it was the bottom of the ninth, the top of the batting order, and the Mets were up. The first man hit a single. The second man bunted and advanced the runner to second base. Then, joy of joys, there was a long hit to left field. The Cubs' outfielder misjudged the ball, and the man at second made it to the plate. Although there was a runner at second again, the pitcher managed to strike out the next two hitters. But it was a new ball game with a tied score, and the game went into extra innings.

Ezra had been sitting on the edge of the sofa during these past innings. Now he relaxed slightly and sat back. He could never describe the feeling of well-being he had when his team was ahead. And tieing up the game in the ninth inning was just as good. There was no change in the score until the Mets were up again in the bottom of the eleventh. The third man up at the plate—it was Dave Kingman—hit a home run. The game was over, and the Mets had won. The season was off to a wonderful start.

The phone rang again. Louis was calling. He and Bruce had been watching the game at their house. The three boys began to analyze it. Suddenly Ezra remembered. "Listen, I've got to get off the phone. My father asked me to go to the post office for him."

Ezra grabbed his jacket and rushed off. His watch showed 5:20. But he thought the post office would be open until six, so he wasn't worried.

He was wrong. The door was locked and the sign outside gave the post-office hours as 8:00 A.M. to 5:00 P.M. Ezra could hear people inside, so he began banging on the door. Perhaps they would open it and sell him the stamps after all. However, the people inside paid no attention. Finally one man came, shook his head, and pointed to his wristwatch. There was no use. Ezra would have to return for the stamps the next day.

"Tomorrow?" bellowed Mr. Feldman, when he came home. "I need those stamps tonight!"

5

EZRA STRIKES OUT

No one can reach the age of ten without having angered his parents at least a few times. But thinking back on his childhood, Ezra couldn't remember ever having done anything that upset his father as much as his failure to buy those stamps.

"You had two hours to walk four blocks," said Mr. Feldman. "How could the post office be closed?"

"I only had an hour," said Ezra, defending himself. "The phone didn't ring till almost four o'clock."

"OK, an hour. How long does it take a boy your size to walk to the post office? A turtle could have been there and back six times! This letter of mine has to get out now so that it will be postmarked before midnight. How can I mail it without stamps?"

"I just wanted to see the end of the baseball game," said Ezra.

He had said the wrong thing. If his father was angry before, the word *baseball* made him still madder. Ezra might as well have waved a red sheet in front of a bull.

"Baseball, baseball, baseball," bellowed Mr. Feldman. "That's all I hear around here. It's a disease with you. If you aren't watching a game on TV, you're listening to a game on the radio."

"But Dad, this was the first game of the new season. I'd been waiting for it for months," protested Ezra. He knew he could never make his father understand. Every boy in his school and most of the girls, too, had run home to watch that same baseball game. None of them had to defend themselves for wanting to see it. Everyone else liked baseball and understood the importance of the first game of the new season. It was unfair that of all the fathers in the world, or at least of all the fathers in Flushing, Ezra had the only one who thought baseball was a waste of time. And now he was in trouble for not getting to the post office on time because of the game!

"When will you learn to put your mind on higher things?" demanded Mr. Feldman.

"Like skyscrapers and elevators, you mean?" asked Ezra.

Mr. Feldman was not in the mood to be diverted by a joke. "Go to your room!" he shouted. "And don't turn on the radio! I don't want to hear the sound of another baseball game in this house. Ever! Do you hear me?"

Of course Ezra heard him, and he was glad to escape to his room. But he was not glad about his punishment. The injustice of it stung him. Why should something as tiny as a postage stamp make anyone so angry?

Ezra had six fraction problems for arithmetic to do and a chapter in his social-studies book to read, but he had left his school books on the living-room floor. He didn't want to go back to the living room for fear of being yelled at by his father again, so he just lay on his bed, feeling sorry for himself and waiting till his mother came home.

Mrs. Feldman started the peace negotiations when she came in from the hospital. She began by coming into Ezra's bedroom and explaining why that single stamp was so important. "Your father just heard of a special grant that he wants to apply for from abroad. He got an application form, but it must be mailed by midnight tonight if he is to be in the running. So the stamp that only cost forty cents may mean that he will lose five thousand dollars."

"How come he only found out about it today?" asked Ezra.

"That's a good question, and I don't know the answer," said Mrs. Feldman. "It's probably the reason why your father is so angry. He should have heard about it before this."

"Maybe he wouldn't have gotten it anyhow," said Ezra. "You don't get everything you apply for." He was remembering the school raffles that he had entered. Once he had invested two dollars for ten tickets, hoping to win his own color television set. But even though he bought ten tickets, he had lost and the winner was a boy whose family already owned three television sets.

"Well, that's true," agreed Mrs. Feldman. "But still you should go to your father later and apologize. This means a great deal to him, and I don't think you understand why he is so angry."

Ezra shrugged his shoulders. He could apologize. But he knew his father would still be angry. And besides, it wasn't his fault that his father hadn't heard about the grant till the very last minute.

"Will I be able to watch the baseball game tomorrow?" asked Ezra. "The season is just beginning, and I don't want to miss the early games."

"We'll see," said Mrs. Feldman. "I'll speak to your father and try to make him understand why they are so important to you."

Mrs. Feldman left the room to carry on phase two of the peace talks.

By supper time a shaky truce had been set up, primarily because Mrs. Feldman remembered Harris's old stamp collection in the closet. A phone call to Princeton had brought the response, "Sure, take any stamps you want." Closer inspection had revealed several new airmail stamps that Mr. Feldman might use.

As the three of them sat around the table eating the meal that Mrs. Feldman had quickly put in and taken out of the microwave oven, Mr. Feldman remembered some other news from his campus. "I got a letter today from the people up at Albany," he said. "They asked me to change the date of my meeting with them next month from the fourteenth to the seventh. So I'll be driving up to see them a week earlier than I planned."

"I have to work that weekend," Mrs. Feldman reminded her husband. "You'd better take Ezra with you."

Ezra and his father exchanged looks. Neither one liked the idea.

"Can't you change your schedule with someone?" asked Mr. Feldman.

"I did. That's why I'm working that weekend. You told me that you would be away on the fourteenth, and so I made a lot of arrangements. And I know that Dr. Clive is going away on the seventh." She thought a moment. "Maybe Ezra can spend the weekend with Bruce and Louis or one of his other friends."

"That's a good idea," said Ezra.

But the evening seemed to be one when everything went wrong. Bruce and Louis and their parents were going to visit relatives that weekend. And Ezra's other friend, David, was scheduled to have his tonsils out that weekend.

"I have another idea," said Mrs. Feldman,

reaching for the phone. For the second time in an hour she dialed Harris's number. She explained the situation to him and asked if Ezra could pay another visit to his brother the weekend of May seventh. Ezra listened to his mother's end of the conversation.

"Oh. Of course. Certainly. I understand. We'll work something out here. Don't worry," she said.

When she hung up, she said, "That's the weekend that Harris is going up to Providence to visit Rosalie." Rosalie, who was Harris's girl friend, was a student at Brown University. Mrs. Feldman shrugged her shoulders. "I've run out of good ideas for the evening," she said.

There seemed to be no alternative to Ezra's accompanying his father. He had done it a couple of times in the past when his father took short trips. But this time Ezra thought he would rather go to the hospital and have his tonsils out instead.

"You'll both have to make the best of it,"

said Mrs. Feldman. "You'll probably have a wonderful time."

Ezra looked at her with surprise. His mother had an incredible imagination, he thought.

Mr. Feldman went to his study to work on the grant application, and Ezra went to his bedroom to work on his fractions. When he turned the light out at 9:30, he could hear a Mozart piano quintet on the radio in the living room. The front door banged as Mr. Feldman went out to mail the application. I hope he gets the grant, Ezra thought. And I hope the Mets get the pennant, he added.

6

AN INCH FROM ALBANY

Although Mr. Feldman did not like baseball or pumpkin pie, he did share one taste with Ezra. They both liked chocolate. Mr. Feldman often reminded them that for three years during the Second World War he had not tasted a single ounce of chocolate. "I always said that when I had the access and the money, I would eat only chocolate for an entire day," Mr. Feldman told Ezra. "The problem is that by the time I was in such a position, I was an adult and knew better." Still, even though he controlled his passion, Mr. Feldman did indulge it from time to time.

Three days after the grant application was mailed (with Harris's stamps affixed to the envelope), Mr. Feldman came home with the news that a new shop specializing in homemade chocolates had opened on Long Island, just a few miles from their home. "Come on, Ezra, let's find out if it is as good as the article in the newspaper says it is."

Ezra got into the car with his father. Chocolate was one thing they couldn't possibly fight about.

Despite the midafternoon traffic, Mr. Feldman remained calm and cheerful both going and returning. The store turned out to be a candy lover's heaven, and they tasted many before making a decision about a purchase. Sitting in the car on the way home, stuffed with chocolate samples, Ezra asked cautiously, "What are your chances for getting the grant that you applied for?"

"Now that the application is filed, they aren't bad," Mr. Feldman admitted. "I won't know anything for at least six months, though." He paused a moment. "I'm sorry that I got so angry at you the other evening. But time was of the essence, and without those

stamps of Harris's, I don't know what I would have done."

Parents are strong on making kids apologize for things, but apologizing themselves happens less often. "That's OK, Dad," Ezra said. And suddenly all the bad taste of Friday evening was gone. The reason wasn't the pound of chocolate-covered apricots in the box on his lap, filling the car with the aroma of the candy shop. Nor was it all the candies he had tasted in the store. Being friends with his father once again was what made the difference.

That evening Mr. Feldman rescinded his order, laid down in the heat of anger, that Ezra was not to watch or listen to any baseball games. Ezra watched and the Mets won. The evening was perfect.

Two weeks later, however, there was another father-and-son clash, and again it was because of baseball. Mr. Feldman walked into Ezra's bedroom at eleven o'clock at night and caught his son listening to a late baseball game when he was supposed to be sound asleep.

"You're taking advantage of me," his father scolded. "I said you could listen, but I didn't say you could listen at this hour of the night. You have school tomorrow!"

"Didn't you ever do anything your parents didn't want you to do when you were a kid?" asked Ezra.

"Yes. I read underneath the bedcovers with a flashlight," said Mr. Feldman. "It was a biography of Napoleon." He paused for a

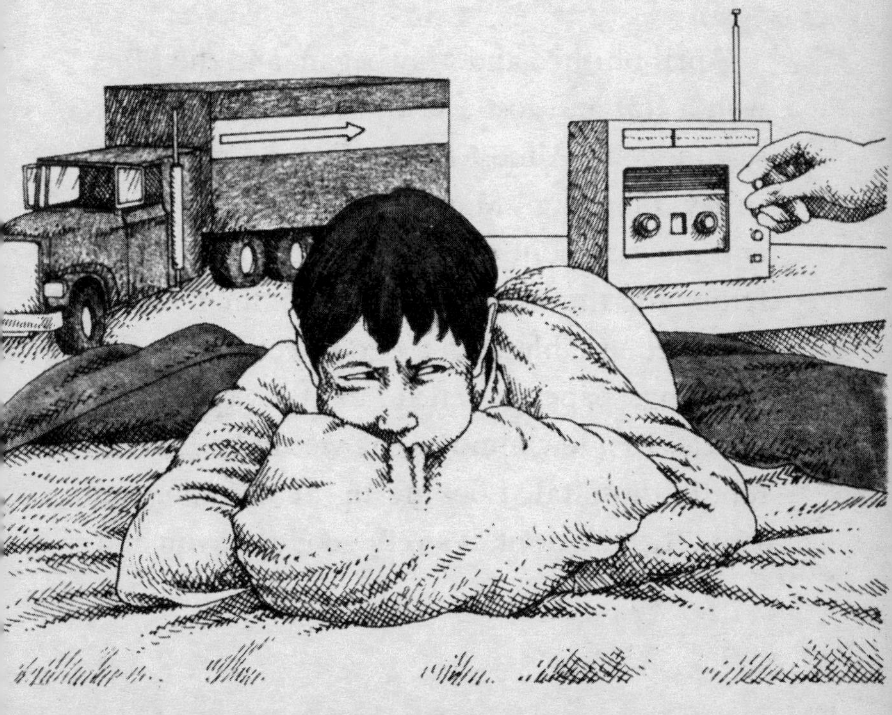

moment. "If I ever catch you doing a thing like that, I'll double your allowance. But listening to this rot"—he nodded toward the radio, which he had already turned off—"there's no excuse for it." Ezra wondered briefly if increasing his allowance by reading about Napoleon in the dark was worth damaging his eyesight. He decided in favor of twenty-twenty vision. He also decided that his father would never understand what baseball meant to him.

April finished and May began, and the Mets won a few and lost a few. That's the way the season went. Almost before Ezra knew it, Saturday morning, May seventh, had arrived, and he was about to go off to Albany with his father for the weekend. Mrs. Feldman sat at the kitchen table with a cup of coffee and the morning paper opened to the crossword puzzle. In a few minutes she would be leaving for the hospital. Looking up at her son, she said, "Ezra, I think it's very good that you and your father are going to spend a little time together this weekend."

Ezra wasn't so sure. He went to his room to get his overnight bag. He opened a drawer to take out a sweat shirt. He had a huge collection of shirts, because every time his father went off on a trip to give a lecture or to attend a conference at a different college or university, he brought home a new shirt for him. The shirts were all different colors, which was nice. They were all different sizes, which was not nice. Mr. Feldman often got confused when he went shopping, and instead of buying a child's size, he sometimes brought home a man's. Ezra had made a game of giving new meanings to the words on the shirts. He looked through them:

YALE
(You Are Large Enough)

COLUMBIA
(Can Only Ladies' Umbrellas
Maim Big Intelligent Alligators)

DARTMOUTH
(Do All Red Tongued Mouths Open Up To Hiss)

"Ezra!" Mr. Feldman called from the next room. "What's keeping you?"

Ezra grabbed his red OHIO STATE (Oh Heavens I Own Seven Thin American Turkey Eggs) and came running. He kissed his mother good-bye. Then he followed his father outside to the car.

"Here," said Mr. Feldman, handing Ezra the road map of New York State. "Study this. You may learn something this weekend." His father was always on the lookout for educational experiences. He didn't seem to believe in doing anything just for fun.

"Do you know how to spell Albany?" Mr. Feldman asked. Then he spelled it out before Ezra could show him that he knew. *"A-l-b-a-n-y."*

Ezra thought of the new shirt he would

probably bring home with him: All Long Books Always Nag You. Carefully he opened the map. After a few minutes, he finally located Albany.

"Did you remember to bring your toothbrush?" asked Mr. Feldman.

Ezra thought for a moment. He realized that he had forgotten his comb, but he did have the toothbrush. "Yes," he said.

His finger slipped and he lost Albany, so he tried to find it again.

"Did you bring a book to read while I'm at my meeting?" asked Mr. Feldman.

This time Ezra didn't even have to think. He knew that he had packed his baseball encyclopedia into his overnight bag. It took up more room than his underwear and clean T-shirt and pajamas. In fact, he had almost had to leave everything else at home in order to pack the huge book.

"I've got something to read," he said.

His finger slipped on the map again, and

he couldn't find Albany. He looked at the names of the cities and towns on that side of the map. Then he made a fantastic discovery.

"Dad," Ezra said. "Did you know that Cooperstown is only an inch away from Albany?"

"What?" asked Mr. Feldman.

"An inch," repeated Ezra. "I've always wanted to go to Cooperstown. Couldn't we stop there?"

"The New York Historical Association is in Cooperstown," said Mr. Feldman. "Since when are you interested in history?"

"I'm interested in baseball history, and Cooperstown is the home of the Baseball Hall of Fame," said Ezra. "Please, Dad, let's go there," he begged.

"I should have known it had something to do with baseball!" Mr. Feldman sighed. "Anyhow, we won't have time to go off our route to other places."

Ezra bit his lip. If he had been clever, he would have said that he wanted to go to the

New York Historical Association, whatever that was. Then, once they got to Cooperstown, he could have found a way to get to the baseball museum. If Bruce and Louis had been going on a trip with their father to a place that was only an inch away from Cooperstown, he knew they would stop there. Why couldn't he have a father who understood and cared about baseball?

For the rest of the ride Ezra and his father hardly exchanged a word. Ezra wondered if his father was nervous about the meeting that he was going to. Mr. Feldman turned on the car radio and listened to the news and some music. Ezra stared out the window. He read the license plates on the cars on the highway. Some of them had messages or words like DIANE, I LUV U, MY CAR, and GEORGE I. When he got tired of looking at the license plates, Ezra studied the map. He added up the little red numbers showing the mileage. He discovered that the inch between Albany and Cooperstown came to sixty-five miles. If they drove fast, they could reach it in an hour. But Ezra knew that when his father had made up his mind about something, it was useless to nag. So he saved his breath and sat silent all the way to Albany.

7

BASEBALLS AND MEATBALLS

By one o'clock Ezra and his father had checked into their room and had a sandwich in the motel coffee shop.

"All right," said Mr. Feldman. "You're on your own for the afternoon. You can read your book or watch TV in the room. I packed the chess computer in with my things in case you want to play with it." He put his hand into his pants pocket and pulled out a couple of quarters. "Here. You can also try the pinball machine in the lounge."

Ezra looked at the two quarters. They

would pay for about six minutes of time on the pinball machine. The afternoon was going to be a long one. He went upstairs to their room and turned on the TV. If he were lucky, there would be a baseball game to watch. Unfortunately, it was raining in New York City and the Yankee game had been called off. The Mets weren't scheduled to play until later in the day, in Houston. There was nothing to watch.

Ezra lay down on his bed with his baseball encyclopedia. He checked out all the statistics for Ty Cobb. Though Cobb had lived and played long before he was born, Ezra liked reading about the old-time baseball players. Ty Cobb had 4,191 base hits in his career—more than anyone else. His lifetime batting average was 367, and he had 892 stolen bases. Ezra flipped the pages of the encyclopedia. It had over 2,000 of them. He would need a long time to learn everything listed there, and he read for a couple of hours until he got a little restless.

For something to do, he went downstairs and bought a candy bar from a machine in the lounge and then returned to the room. He tried the television set again, but there was nothing that looked interesting. Finally, from boredom, he went to his father's overnight bag and took out the chess game. He plugged it in and set it for the simplest level.

The machine could play chess at five different grades ranging from the simple to the more and more difficult. At the simplest level it would answer Ezra's move within five seconds. At the hardest level the machine needed many hours to "think." Ezra moved first. The machine moved. Unlike his father, the machine silently blinked its responses without making comments like, "That was a foolish move." If the machine thought Ezra was stupid, it kept the news to itself.

Ezra lost the first two games he played with the machine. He was about to begin a third one when the phone rang. His father was checking up on him.

"I'll meet you in the lobby in twenty minutes," said Mr. Feldman. "Then we'll go off somewhere to dinner."

"OK," said Ezra. "How's the meeting going?"

"Not so good," admitted Mr. Feldman. "We've been covering the same ground all afternoon, and we seem to be getting nowhere.

They can't decide whether or not to set up the lecture series that I'm proposing."

At 6:20, Ezra got ready to meet his father. He washed his face and hands, because he could imagine his father asking him if he had done so. Without a comb, he smoothed his hair with his fingers. He didn't want his appearance to annoy his father. Mr. Feldman seemed to be batting zero these days. First there had been the tension about the grant, and now the lecture series seemed to be going foul. Ezra knew his father's humor would not be improved by this afternoon's meeting. He took out his Ohio State sweat shirt and put it on. It was a man's large, and so even with cuffs the sleeves hung below his wrists. Ezra went downstairs and found his father waiting for him.

"At least we'll have a good dinner," said Mr. Feldman. "I heard of an Italian restaurant a couple of miles from here. Imagine coming all this way just for a plate of Italian food."

Ezra wanted to suggest that if they went to Cooperstown on the way home, the trip wouldn't be wasted. But he knew better than to upset his father. Instead, he asked, "Why do you think they haven't made a decision about your lecture series?"

"It's very simple," Mr. Feldman explained. "It's a way of exercising power. Professor Strauss, who is the committee chairman, controls the money. The minute he makes a decision about this series, he is handing over money and power to someone else. So for the moment, he's enjoying himself. It's a capricious act on his part. Tomorrow he can just as easily change his mind."

Ezra felt proud to have his father speak so seriously with him. He didn't know the word *capricious,* but he thought he understood what his father was saying. "Sometimes baseball managers act like that," he said. "If a manager has a fight with a player, he might keep him out of a game, even though he might hit a home run or make a great catch. A good manager doesn't use his power that way."

"Exactly," said Mr. Feldman. "But that's why they say that power corrupts." Ezra smiled at his father. They didn't often agree on something, but when they did, it felt very good.

When they arrived at the restaurant, it was crowded with Saturday evening diners. They got the last empty table, close to the entrance door.

"Well, at least we got a place," said Ezra.

Mr. Feldman ordered himself a drink. Then they studied the menus. "Ossi Buchi alla Milanese" Mr. Feldman told the waitress, when she came to their table. Everything on the menu had a long and unfamiliar name.

"I just want spaghetti," said Ezra.

"Spaghetti con Salsa Semplice di Pomodoro e Polpette," his father told the waitress.

Mr. Feldman drank his scotch, and Ezra sipped a Coke as they sat waiting. Suddenly

Mr. Feldman jumped up. "Strauss!" he called out.

Ezra saw an elderly man with a heavy white moustache and thick eyeglasses standing at the doorway of the restaurant.

"Hello, Feldman," said the old man. "No wonder I can't find a seat. If you knew to come here, then the whole place must be filled with out-of-towners."

"Please, join us," urged Mr. Feldman.

"'I guess I have no choice if I don't want to starve," the old man answered. Ezra thought he didn't sound very polite, but he noticed that Professor Strauss was quick to sit at their table.

"Strauss, I'd like you to meet my son Ezra," said Mr. Feldman. "Ezra, this is Professor Laurence Strauss of the history department here. He's one of the men I spent the afternoon with."

Ezra tried to look friendly, even though the man had been giving his father such a hard time.

The two men began conversing, and Ezra let his mind wander. The waitress came with the food for Ezra and his father. The steam rising from it smelled delicious. No wonder there was now a line of people standing in the lobby waiting for seats.

Ezra was starved, and so he stabbed one of the little meatballs with his fork and lifted it to his mouth.

"Well, young man, what are your interests?" asked the professor.

Ezra was not expecting to be addressed, and he started at the question. His hand shook, and the meatball fell from his fork and slid down into the wide sleeve of his sweat shirt.

It was a terrible moment. The meatball burned his arm, and Ezra blushed as red as the tomato sauce on his plate. He wondered if his father and Professor Strauss had noticed the mishap. He wanted to cry out from the burn and slide under the table with embarrassment. Instead, he said and did nothing.

"He has baseball fever," said Mr. Feldman, answering for his son. "One of these days I hope he'll learn that there are a few other things in the world besides baseball."

Ezra always felt bad when his father spoke about him that way, as if he were an idiot or something. But now, with the burning meatball in his sleeve, he didn't care what he said. He was too busy trying to shake out the meatball secretly. Holding his arm under the table, he moved it inside his shirt. Luckily the large sleeve that had caught the meatball now released it, and the meatball slid out onto the floor. Ezra felt as relieved as if he were safe at home plate.

"What team do you root for?" asked the professor.

"The Mets," said Ezra.

"You're crazy! You look too intelligent for that nonsense," said the professor. "You should use your time more constructively."

"That's what I always tell him. If I've told him once, I've told him a hundred times that

baseball is just a waste of time," Mr. Feldman agreed.

"The Mets haven't a chance in the world," said the professor. "I would have thought you would root for the Yankees."

"You never can tell what will happen," said Ezra. "This is a new season. Did you know that one year the Yankees won three World Series games with scores of sixteen-three, twelve-nothing, and ten-nothing, and they still lost the series?"

The professor nodded his head. "That was in 1960, when Pittsburgh won," he said. "Still the odds are against the Mets. Do you realize how many times the Yankees have won the World Series?" he asked Ezra.

"Sure," said Ezra. "In 1923, '27, '28, '32, '36, '37, '39, '41, '43—"

"Enough, enough," said Professor Strauss.

Ezra wondered why he didn't want to hear about 1947, '49, '50, '51, '52, '53. . . .

"Do you know who won the series in 1924?"

asked Professor Strauss, interrupting Ezra's thoughts.

"The Senators," said Ezra, grinning. He was having fun.

The waitress brought the professor his food. "Who managed the St. Louis Cardinals to their first pennant in 1926?" he asked Ezra.

"Rogers Hornsby," said Ezra with a smile. This was a game he often played with Bruce and Louis. They asked one another baseball questions and tried to see who knew the most. Ezra almost always won.

"Your son is brilliant," said Professor Strauss, turning to Mr. Feldman. "His memory is phenomenal for a boy his age." He turned to Ezra. "How old are you? Twelve?"

"I'm ten. My birthday was last month," said Ezra. "I got *The Baseball Encyclopedia* for my birthday, and I've been doing a lot of reading in it," he said by way of explanation. He didn't want the professor to think that he always knew so much.

"Incredible! This boy will go far. He has an excellent mind. You must be very proud of him," said Professor Strauss.

"Of course I am," said Mr. Feldman, looking rather surprised at the professor's praise of his son. "But he doesn't seem to have any other interests besides baseball."

"That's a sign of intelligence. Concentration in one area is excellent. And someday he will surprise you by transferring his interest, his concentration, and his memory skills to some other totally different area of study."

"Really?" Mr. Feldman seemed stunned by the way the conversation was going. "I'm surprised that you are so knowledgeable about baseball," he said.

"There's nothing like baseball to take your mind off the problems of the world," said Professor Strauss. "It probably kept me sane during the forties and fifties, to say nothing of the sixties and seventies." He turned to Ezra. "Have you told your father about the correlation between the World Series and the presidential elections?"

"What are you talking about?" asked Mr. Feldman.

"From 1908 to 1976, in every presidential election year that the American League won the World Series, the Republican nominee won the election. And when a National League team won the series, then the Democratic candidate won."

"Then in 1980, when Reagan was elected—" began Mr. Feldman.

"The Philadelphia Phillies in the National League won the series," said the professor.

"But Reagan is a Republican," pointed out Mr. Feldman.

"Yes. It was a fascinating coincidence while it lasted," Professor Strauss said. "Tell me," he asked, "have you been to Cooperstown?"

"No," said Ezra. "It's too far off our route."

"Nonsense," said the professor with authority. "It's only an hour and a half from here. I insist that you go," he said, turning to Mr. Feldman. "You'll be surprised at how interesting it is."

He paused a moment. "I'll tell you what. Let's cancel the meeting we scheduled for tomorrow morning. I want more time to think over some of the things you said today. You had some good ideas, but I'm not quite ready to make any decisions. And you can use the time to take your son to Cooperstown."

Mr. Feldman looked surprised. He had anticipated a Yes or a No the following morning. Instead, he found himself agreeing to take Ezra to Cooperstown, the home of the Baseball Hall of Fame. The development wasn't what he had expected.

Ezra was surprised too. "Great!" he said. "I measured the distance to Cooperstown with my knuckle. It's only an inch from Albany," he informed the professor.

Then he turned to tackle his remaining meatballs and spaghetti. After baseballs, he liked meatballs next best.

8

THE BASEBALL HALL OF FAME

"Who would have thought I would be driving to Cooperstown?" Mr. Feldman said the next morning, as they started on their way. What he was really thinking, Ezra imagined, was who would have thought a man like Professor Strauss would care about baseball.

The person who was driving Ezra to the Baseball Hall of Fame on Sunday morning was very different from the one who had driven him to Albany the day before. The dinner and conversation with Professor Strauss had completely changed Mr. Feldman's mood.

He whistled as he drove, and when he spoke, his voice was cheerful.

Ezra was delighted that they were heading toward Cooperstown. He hoped the professor would agree to his father's lecture series. He tried to think of something to say or do to show his appreciation to his father. Then he remembered what Harris had said about how pleased his father would be if Ezra played chess with him more often.

"Dad," said Ezra, "yesterday afternoon, while you were at your meeting, I played a couple of games on the chess computer."

"How did you make out?" asked Mr. Feldman.

"I lost," said Ezra. "But it was fun. I bet I could beat that machine one of these days."

"I bet you could too, if you played more," said Mr. Feldman.

"Do you think I'll ever beat you?" asked Ezra.

"You might," conceded his father, "but only if you work at it."

"Dad, if I beat you at a game of chess, will you come with me to see a live game at Shea Stadium?"

Mr. Feldman laughed. "Here I am driving you to a baseball museum, of all places, and as if that isn't enough you want me to take you to a baseball game too," said Mr. Feldman. But his voice wasn't angry. He sounded amused.

"Well, will you?" asked Ezra. "If I beat you, of course."

"Sure. You beat me at a game of chess, and I'll take you to a two-timer. No, what do they call it when they play two games one right after the other?"

"Doubleheader," Ezra corrected his father. "It's a deal!" Ezra knew they had made a real agreement, and he felt very good.

"This is a funny, out-of-the-way place to have a baseball museum" Mr. Feldman commented, as they approached Cooperstown.

"It's here because it's also the home of

Abner Doubleday. Some people say that he invented baseball," Ezra explained to his father.

They parked their car between one with a license plate from Michigan and another with plates from Florida.

"Imagine! People seem to travel here from all over the country," Mr. Feldman marveled aloud. This observation didn't surprise Ezra at all.

Inside, the museum was like a treasure chest full of wonderful things for Ezra to see. There were huge enlarged photographs of all the record-making events in baseball history. And enclosed in glass cases were the very balls and gloves and uniforms that had taken part in the major events of the game.

Ezra didn't know which way to look first, whether to start upstairs and work his way down or downstairs and work his way up. He wanted to be everywhere at once, seeing everything at the same time.

Ezra and Mr. Feldman waited while a family

of six people read an inscription, and when they moved on, they were able to see the locker in which Stan Musial of the Cardinals had stored his uniform. There was a glass door on the locker so Ezra could look inside and see Musial's old uniform with the number six on it. Musial's old playing shoes were there too, worn and dirty. They looked as if any moment the baseball player would return and put them on.

"Look! There's the bat Musial used when he became the first major-league player to hit five home runs in a double header," Ezra read aloud. "It was on May 2, 1954."

"May 2, 1954," said Mr. Feldman. "That was the day Prime Minister Jawaharlal Nehru of India concluded his first Asian conference with the rulers from Ceylon, Pakistan, Burma, and Indonesia."

Ezra looked at his father with amazement. How could somebody say so many words in English and not make a single bit of sense? He didn't know what his father was talking about.

Then he remembered how often his father had said the very same thing to him when he tried to explain a baseball game to him.

"It's amazing," said Mr. Feldman. "Who remembers that conference now?"

Mr. Feldman was still thinking about India, and as far as Ezra knew India didn't have a single baseball team.

"Oh, look at that!" Ezra said, pointing to still another exhibit. "That baseball is really old. It's the ball from opening day at the Polo Grounds on April 12, 1911."

"April 12, 1911," mused Mr. Feldman. "That was the fiftieth anniversary of the firing on Fort Sumter. It was the beginning of the Civil War."

"Oh, Dad! When people are at a baseball game, they don't think about wars and killing," Ezra protested.

"Now that was a real tragedy," said a gray-haired man to Mr. Feldman. Ezra thought he was talking about Fort Sumter, but the man was pointing to an enlarged photograph of

NY

the old Giants team leaving the field after the final game at the Polo Grounds on September 29, 1957.

"Imagine! They pulled down the stadium and built apartment houses there in its place," said the man. "New York was never the same after the Giants left," he said sadly.

"What about the Dodgers?" asked another man, who had overheard him. "There never was and there never will be another team like those old Brooklyn Dodgers."

People gathered around and began debating the merits of the New York Giants and the Brooklyn Dodgers. Ezra wanted to listen to them, but he was worried that his father would insist upon relating some historic event that took place on September 29, 1957. Imagine having a father who spoke as if he were a cross between a newspaper and a history book. Ezra didn't think that the baseball fans would understand. He pulled his father away from the discussion and toward some old benches from the Polo Grounds and from Ebbetts Field.

There was a picture of Harvey Haddix of the Pittsburgh Pirates. He had pitched the first twelve-inning, no-hit perfect game against the Braves at Milwaukee on May 26, 1959.

Mr. Feldman read the caption under the picture. Ezra waited for the computer inside his father's head to respond. In a way, his father's brain was like the electronic chess set. He had programed himself to think in terms of world history. His photographic memory reacted automatically. Sure enough, within seven seconds Mr. Feldman said, "Why that's just two days after John Foster Dulles died. He was Secretary of State under President Eisenhower."

"President Eisenhower was a baseball fan," said Ezra. "He always threw out the first ball at the beginning of the baseball season, and he attended games whenever he could. I've seen pictures of him."

"I wonder why he bothered doing a thing like that," said Mr. Feldman.

"It's probably the reason he wanted to become president in the first place," said Ezra. "All presidents are invited to throw out the first ball, and it's one of the best jobs they get to do. They sit in box seats in the very front, and they can shake hands with all the players." He thought for a moment. "If I don't become a baseball statistician, maybe I'll become president of the United States."

"That," said Mr. Feldman, "I've got to live to see."

9

EZRA, THE ROOKIE CHESS PLAYER

The baseball season was in full swing. Every day new games were played and new records were made all over the country. The newspapers were filled with photographs and news articles. Ezra went to his birthday doubleheader with Bruce and Louis. The Mets won one game and lost one game. The outcome could have been worse. Attending the game, Ezra thought about his baseball-chess bargain with his father.

Two weeks after they returned from Albany Mr. Feldman received a letter from

Professor Strauss accepting his proposal. So now Mr. Feldman was very busy. He was home just as many hours as in the past, but much of his time was spent writing letters to others and notes to himself about the lecture series that was to take place the following autumn. He was so busy that he didn't notice when Ezra stayed up past eleven o'clock on a school night to watch the end of a baseball game.

Mrs. Feldman had said, "Ezra, will you be able to get out of bed tomorrow morning?"

"Sure," said Ezra.

"OK, then just this once," his mother said. She was very easygoing. Ezra hoped she wouldn't be too disappointed when he grew up and didn't win those famous prizes that Harris had told him about.

But Ezra was determined that he would win a chess game from his father. On evenings when there wasn't a baseball game, he often played a couple of games against the chess computer. The machine kept beating him, but Ezra didn't worry. It was a secret between the two of them. Besides, the machine let him think as long as he wanted to. Ezra would try out several positions until he found the one that seemed the strongest. And then, when he decided what to do, he entered his moves into the machine and waited for its response.

One evening Ezra won two games in a row against the machine. Of course, it was set at the simplest level, but still beating it gave him confidence. He went to his father. "How about a game of chess?" he asked.

Mr. Feldman looked up from his notes. "As a matter of fact, I'm ready for a break," he said. So the two of them sat at the dining-room table with the chessboard between them. It was the first game they had played together in a long time. "Don't forget, if I win, you're going to take me to a baseball game," Ezra reminded his father.

"Sure," his father said. He picked up a black pawn and a white pawn in his hands and held them behind his back. Ezra chose the right hand. It held the white pawn, which meant that Ezra would go first. This way of deciding was fair. If they decided the way they did at a baseball game, his father would never be first, since this was his house. In chess, unlike baseball, the player who goes first has an advantage.

Ezra moved. And then his father. Playing a game against a real person wasn't easy. You had to keep wondering what they thought of what you did. And Mr. Feldman usually said out loud what he thought. "That's a foolish move. You left your queen unprotected," he said.

What was worse, serious chess players always insist upon "touch move," which means that whatever piece you touch has to be moved, even if in the midst of the move you have a better idea. In baseball, if the pitcher winds up for a pitch and then doesn't throw the ball to the batter, it is considered a balk.

Ezra could see the sense of the rule in baseball, but not in chess. Often when he played with his father the touch-move rule cost him the game. He would put his hand out and start to move a piece and then suddenly see a better move. It was too late. "You touched the rook," Mr. Feldman would remind him. "Now you've got to move it." The chess machine never noticed if Ezra touched a piece and then changed his mind. No wonder it was easier to win against a machine than against his father. They played two games, and Ezra lost them both.

"Keep practicing," his father said, as they

put the chess pieces back into their box. "If you don't beat me this year, maybe you'll beat me next."

That was no consolation to Ezra. He was determined to get a win before the current baseball season ended.

A few days later Harris phoned to speak to his parents. He had registered for two summer courses so he was still in Princeton, even though it was July.

Mr. and Mrs. Feldman had gone to a concert, and so Ezra and Harris had a long conversation together. The Dodge was up to 143,500 miles. "I drove to Rhode Island one weekend, and Roger drove to Cambridge the next," said Harris. "But mostly, when we don't feel like studying, we just drive around and around here."

"Isn't the gas awfully expensive?" Ezra asked.

"It sure is," agreed Harris. "Why do you think I always call collect?"

They spoke some more. Of course Harris

already knew about things like the successful trip to Albany and the trip to the Baseball Hall of Fame. "I lost two chess games to Dad the other evening," admitted Ezra. "I don't think I'll ever beat him. Especially when he plays touch move."

"That always did me in too," Harris remembered. "He's very strict about it because a good chess player thinks with his head and not with his fingers. You should be able to visualize the board without having to move pieces around to see what they will look like."

"I know," Ezra said. "But my hand always seems to shoot out before I can stop it."

"Right," Harris sympathized. "I don't remember how I trained myself to control it."

Two days later Harris remembered, and he sent Ezra a letter. The letter contained only one sentence—not even "Dear Ezra" or "love, Harris"—just one sentence, four words long. But it was very important, and it was the turning point in Ezra's chess career. The sentence said: "Sit on your hands."

The idea was so simple that Ezra was amazed that it hadn't occurred to him earlier. Now whenever he played chess, even with the machine, he sat on his hands until he was absolutely ready to move. If he made a bad move, at least it was the bad move he wanted to make and not one he was forced into because he had thought with his fingers. Ezra decided it was like thinking out loud when you answered a question quickly at school. Sometimes you might say the right thing, but more often you wished you had kept your mouth shut.

Ezra lost the next few games he played against his father, but not once was he forced to make a move because he had accidentally or deliberately touched a piece he hadn't intended to move. And then, on the first Sunday in August, on a day when heavy rains cancelled baseball games in seven states, Ezra sat down to play still another chess game with his father.

Ezra chose white once again, and so he

opened with the first move. The next few moves were routine, but then Ezra sacrificed his knight. He permitted his father to take the piece when it could have been avoided, the same way a baseball player makes a sacrifice hit in order to advance a base runner.

"Why did you do that?" asked Mr. Feldman, as he took the knight. "Now you are behind a piece."

However, two days before the chess computer had made that same move when Ezra was playing with it. At the time, Ezra had wondered about the move too. It was an unusual one. And yet, within a few more moves, the machine had won the game. Now Mr. Feldman made the same move that Ezra had made two days before. Ezra copied what the machine had done. Again the game was over within a few moves, and this time Ezra was the winner.

"I can't believe it," said Mr. Feldman. "That was so clever! Let me see it again." He rearranged the pieces on the board and then quickly replayed the white and black moves. "I went here, you went here, I went here, you went here. . . ." he mumbled to himself.

"Ezra, that was brilliant! I would never have thought of that sequence of moves."

"I learned it from the machine," admitted Ezra. "But it counts as winning, doesn't it?"

"It sure does!" Mr. Feldman beamed and held out his hand to shake Ezra's.

"Why are you sitting on your hands?" he asked.

"Oh, it's just a trick I learned from Harris," said Ezra, as he shook hands with his father.

Mrs. Feldman looked up from her Sunday crossword puzzle. "I knew you would do it." She smiled at Ezra.

"Did you know that now Dad is going to take me to a baseball game?" asked Ezra, smiling proudly.

"In the rain?" asked both his parents together.

"Not in the rain. But the next sunny home game," said Ezra. "I'll teach you how to become a baseball fan," he promised.

10

MR. FELDMAN, THE ROOKIE BASEBALL FAN

"I'll be glad to explain everything to you again," offered Ezra the afternoon they went to the baseball game together. He thought he had probably explained the game a dozen times over the past couple of years. Perhaps now his father was ready to understand.

"Not now," said Mr. Feldman. "I want to look around." He watched the people entering the ball park. He was fascinated to see that there were people of all ages and ethnic backgrounds in the stadium. "This is a wonderful cross section of American society," he said to Ezra.

Ezra had been thinking how best to describe the game to his father. He hit on the idea of comparing baseball to a game of chess. Each player, like each chessman, had certain moves to make. He tried to draw a chart comparing the pitchers on each baseball team to the kings. Then he decided that it would be better to compare the pitchers to the queens. After all, in some games there might be several pitchers, and queens could be replaced. But there is only one king. Perhaps the king would be equivalent to a manager. On the other hand, sometimes managers get thrown out of the game by the umpire. Ezra decided that he was just confusing himself. He would probably confuse his father too. So instead, he watched the players as they warmed up. He was happy to be at the game, and he hoped his father would enjoy it too.

Mr. Feldman didn't look at the field at all.

"Do you mind if I ask you a few questions?" he said to a man on his left. "How often do you attend games, and how many games do you watch on TV?"

"What are you, a nut or something?" asked the man.

"No, no. I'm a historian with an interest in sociology," explained Mr. Feldman.

The man didn't seem to understand the difference, but eventually Mr. Feldman was able to engage him in conversation. He talked with him for a long time and took many notes. Then he offered to go and buy Ezra a hot dog. "Don't bother, Dad," said Ezra. "The game is just about to begin, and you don't want to miss any of it. Besides, they'll be coming around to sell them to us right here in a little while."

Nevertheless, Mr. Feldman went downstairs to get hot dogs. He returned with two of them and some information that he found astounding. "Do you know," he said, "I saw people watching the game and listening to it on portable radios at the same time!"

"Sure," said Ezra, "lots of people do that, so they can hear the descriptions of all the plays. Look over there." He pointed to a man sitting across the aisle.

"I can't believe it!" Mr. Feldman was stunned. The man had a small, battery-powered television set.

"Why does he bother to come?" Mr. Feldman asked Ezra. "I must go and interview him."

"No, Dad," said Ezra, "don't bother him. He won't want to talk during the game. He wants the TV set so he can see the instant replays of close calls."

"What is that?" asked Mr. Feldman. "This game is so complicated! But it speaks well of American intelligence that all these people can follow what is going on."

He sat staring at the field. Sometimes Ezra cheered. Sometimes he clapped his hands in rhythm and shouted, "We want a hit!" Some-

times Ezra groaned. Ezra explained that the Mets were losing.

Mr. Feldman wrote quietly through it all. He filled page after page in his notebook. "I think I'll write an article about this," he said.

"No, Dad, you can't possibly write anything until you understand what is going on."

"You're right," agreed Mr. Feldman. "But I'll stick with it until I understand. There must be a reason why people pay good money to sit here. As soon as I understand it, I'll write about it—from a sociological point of view of course."

During the seventh-inning stretch, Mr. Feldman tried to interview a young couple sitting in front of them. The fellow was wearing a shirt that said M.I.T. (Monsters in Trousers, thought Ezra).

"You look as if you've had some education," Mr. Feldman said. "Perhaps you can explain why you would spend a Sunday sitting here watching all this." He waved his hand toward the playing area.

Instead of taking offense, as Ezra feared, the young man said, "When I watch a baseball game, it's all that matters. I don't have to worry about pollution, inflation, recession, communism, cancer, crime, or anything else. All I do is watch the ball." He looked at Mr. Feldman, who was writing down the words as fast as he could.

"Mister, you'd be a happier person if you threw away your pen and just watched that ball."

Mr. Feldman tried. From time to time, during the weeks that followed, he sat down beside Ezra as he watched a game on television. And Ezra, to show his appreciation of his father's new attitude toward baseball, continued to offer to play him a game of chess. After his one loss to his son, Mr. Feldman beat him as before, but Ezra didn't mind as much as he used to. And he noticed that his father had to work a little harder to get his win these days.

So by the time October rolled around that

year, life was a whole new ball game for Ezra. Mr. Feldman had received a letter notifying him that he was awarded the grant that he had applied for in the spring. To celebrate, the Feldmans had dined at Chopmeat Charlie's, and that night even Ezra had steak.

The Mets had a good reason to celebrate too. They weren't in last place the way they'd often been in the past. This year they were in next-to-last place. It was an improvement. Mr. Feldman still didn't understand baseball. Yet he was trying harder to understand Ezra. He was much more relaxed about the time his son spent watching, thinking, and talking about baseball. He stopped complaining about Ezra's baseball-card collection, which now filled three shoe boxes.

Sometimes, to show that he was interested, he would come up to Ezra and ask, "Any FBI's lately?"

"FBI?" asked Ezra. "Don't you mean RBI?"

"What about the grand bangs?" asked Mr.

Feldman, realizing that he had made another error.

"Grand slams," corrected Ezra. He smiled.

Mr. Feldman still didn't like pumpkin pie either.

"It's all right," Mrs. Feldman explained to her son. "It makes the world a much more interesting place if people have different interests and different tastes. Besides, this way there is more pie for you and me."

"And Harris, if he comes home," said Ezra.

"The important thing," she added, "is that you try to understand and respect each other, not whether you understand baseball or history or whatever."

Ezra realized that his father might never learn to understand and *speak* baseball. But as long as he didn't make fun of it, it wouldn't matter. Like speaking Greek, Ezra thought, some people could do it and some couldn't.

And when the baseball season ended that year, Ezra decided that he would read a book of chess openings. He had a good memory, like his father, and it would be the beginning of something new. Reading about chess would be something to pass the time till the next baseball season.